D0247379

Disney

FROZEN II

Anna, Elsa and the Secret River

By Andria Warmflash Rosenbaum

Illustrated by Denise Shimabukuro & Maria Elena Naggi

AUTUMN PUBLISHING

One night, Elsa and Anna's mother sang them a lullaby about a secret white river flowing with answers to the past.

Anna pretended to sleep.
Elsa had just closed her eyes
and **drifted off** when...

... Anna shook her awake.

"**Let's go** find the white river!"

"Let it go," said Elsa. "It's time to sleep."

"But I have a million questions," said Anna, "and the **white river** could have all the answers."

"And don't you wonder why you have **magic**?"

At that, Elsa sat up.

"Let's go!"

It didn't take them long to slip out of the castle and into the forest.

"How will we find the white river?" asked Anna.

"We've got to use our eyes," said Elsa.

"Look!" shouted Anna. "I think I see it!"

The sisters ran towards a

gleaming reflection...

But it was only a **stream**.

"Now what?" asked Anna.

"A stream can lead to a river," said Elsa.

But the stream only led to a **pond**.

"Maybe if we **listen** we'll find the white river," said Elsa. Anna heard the sound of **rushing water**.

They **raced** to meet the river!

But all they found was a **boulder** with **wind** rushing through it.
"If only we could smell the white river," said Anna.
"What would it smell like?" asked Elsa.
"Answers," said Anna, "and...

“... reindeer?”

“This is ridiculous,” said Elsa.

The sisters had used
their **eyes**, their **ears**
and their **noses**.
They still hadn't found
the white river, but
they kept trying.

"I can't see a thing,"
said Anna.
"Try looking out the
other end," said Elsa.

As the hours passed,

Anna and Elsa grew **tired**.

They continued to explore. Elsa found an **old shield** glinting in the moonlight. **"I thought we were close,"** said Anna. They felt like giving up.

Suddenly, the wind **lifted** Anna.
Its power took the girls by surprise.
Something caught Anna's eye!

The wind gently returned Anna to the ground. The sisters raced towards the **white river**...

... but it was only an **ice mountain** glittering in the breaking dawn.

"It's almost morning," said Elsa.

"But we didn't find the white river," said Anna. "**Now** what do we do?"

"**Sleep,**" said Elsa.
Suddenly, the girls were
snug again in their bed.

In the morning, Anna shook Elsa awake.
"Let's go find the white river!"
"It's only in a **lullaby,"** said Elsa.
But then... she wondered if their
adventure had all been a **dream**.